{~Objects~}

M. L. Johnson

mljohnsonauthor.com

ISBN: 978-0-578-70814-0

Debut novel *The Anam Cara Trials*(Working Title)
by M. L. Johnson coming soon.

Contents

Chapter 1

{~Life~}

HELP

{~The Ladder~}

This is not my descent into madness. I've been down here all along. This is my brief message to the surface and to the light to show you what it's like down here in the dark.

This expression can take many forms. Some people drink an entire bottle and get behind a wheel. Some grab a rifle and head to an audience and let the bullets give a speech on their behalf. Some are so fed up and tired of the depths they turn themselves into a human pinata, swinging by their necks, never having to touch the bottom again. But none of those options suit me. All of those are from people who have given up. They have convinced themselves they belong down here or they try to blame anyone but themselves. But not me. I'm just waiting; biding my time. Writing meaningless words on a piece of paper to keep my mind from running away from me and getting lost in the darkness.

One day the ladder will come sliding down to me and I will finally climb up out of the madness. But, are you actually mad if you realize you are? Can I dub myself insane or is that in and of itself too much of a sane and rational thought for the insane to have?

Whatever the case, I don't belong here. My time is coming.

There will be no grand gesture. No pathetic act to make the world "*remember my name.*" Just a silent merger. Another sheep slipping into the camouflage of the herd. I've lived with the wolves long enough.

M. L. Johnson

{~The Polaroid~}

I won't smile for your cheese
I don't want them to see me lying
It's not that I'm particularly sad
I just don't have much to smile about

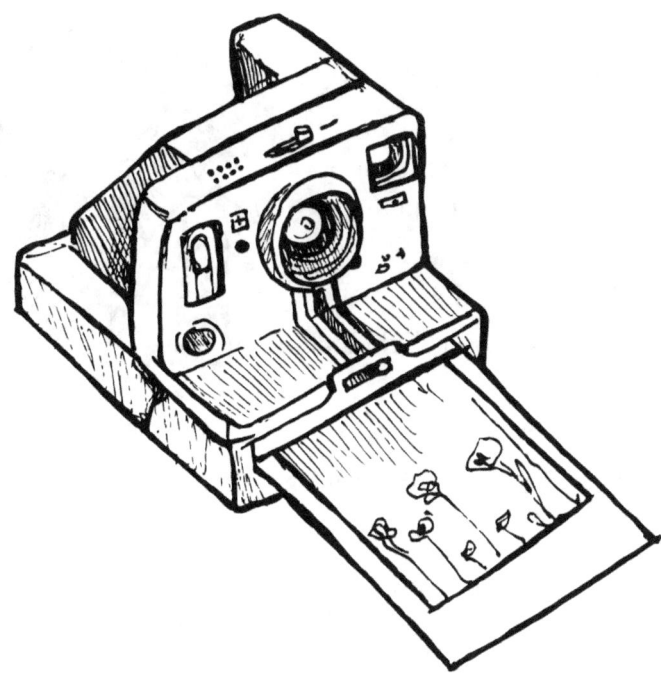

{~The Tide~}

It really is quite concerning
This endless craving and longful yearning

All the candles I left burning
Searching for the answers, but still learning

Between you and I
It was the land and the sky

The sun and the moon
A flower and it's bloom

The pull of the tides
The darkness the light hides

So obvious, yet so veiled
Only in you, the conclusions were held

{~The Monster~}

Truth be told
There was never any truth in what you told

You would say the sun sets in the east
just to make me look in the wrong direction

You would tell me the monsters can't get me in my
sleep if I never close my eyes

You would tell me it's better to swim, just so you could
keep the boat

You didn't care who it hurt
You just wanted someone else to have to find ways to
alleviate the pain alongside you

Someone around to give you a reason to hold in your
tears
Then slowly drown them in yours when they got used
to the taste of salt from their own

Someone to join you in the flames as you watched the
world burn all around you

Only thing is,
two sacks of sh*t are never better than one

Unless you're a manure salesman, or a fly

-     To an old "friend."

{~The Clock~}

We all have one in our pockets, on our wrists, in our cars, on our desks, on our computers, on every appliance, and hanging on every wall in every room of our house. The clock is inescapable and unavoidable. All it takes is one small movement of our eyes and there another one will be, staring us in the face.

"F**k you," the clock says when it meets our gaze.

They are not kind. They show no mercy. They do not care about the color of your skin or what continent you live on. They are the ever-whispering demon, always perched on your shoulder. The healer of all wounds but the creator of all scars. The creepy painting of the old lady that no matter how you view it her eyes follow you across the room.

Each tick is another tock you will never get back from the clock.

"F**k you," the clock says. "Those ticks and those tocks are mine now."

If you have acquired some wealth you can purchase a few more tocks from the clock but in the end they go right back into his greedy little pocket. It's quite sad because the clock is all in our heads. We made up the clock to tell us when we should be expecting our pimples and then our wrinkles.

31,536,000 seconds, 525,600 minutes, 8760 hours.

"Happy Birthday! But also, f**k you!" screams the clock.

Each tick-tock he whispers into our ear is just another reminder of what we haven't done. Another second passed that we haven't visited that beach, climbed that mountain, or jumped out of that plane. The clock stops for no one. The overlord of all existence. The clock is just a figment of our imagination, yet somehow is the most real thing possible.

"F**k you," the clock says.

"Thank you," I reply. For reminding me to never waste a single tick or a single tock that you have given me, beautifully ugly clock.

Why did you lie at the end there?
I don't know.
Felt like they needed at least
one feel good ending.

M. L. Johnson

{~The Track~}

A beaten down car stuck riding the track.
Always in motion but not always intact.
Round and round; never ending.
The vicious cycle; spinning, unbending.
Just one lap; a change of scenery.
Fall in line; shoved along obscenely.
Just one lap; a different layout.
Even with hard work; no way-out.
One more circle and I swear I'll scream.
A silence in the monotony; just a daydream.
Perpetual motion; is there even a choice?
Scream all I want; sewn lips, no voice.
Cement tires slowly exhausting.
Each new rotation even more daunting.
Invoke a pile up just to see some hysteria.
Entire track; disaster area.
Even through the smoke, and through the fire.
Must soldier on; no time to admire.
Covered in dents; broken parts to sever.
But the race carries on, forever and ever.

{~The Painting~}

Life is like looking at a painting.
Having your own thoughts and emotions conjured up
by the different shapes and colors.
Only to have someone walk up to you and tell you that
what you're feeling is wrong.
It's not their place to say,
but they will do it anyway...

And you will listen.

{~The Starbird Rainbowlion~}

Here is a story about a f**king weird lion. Deal with it.

Once upon a time, there lived a young and very curiously unique lion. All of the other lions in his pride and all the others across the entire land were all a crisp golden tan. But, this one particular lion had a bright coat of rainbow striped fur like that of a reverse colored zebra. He was an outcast. Shunned to live away from the pride most of the time. His mother and father made him stay far back from all the hunts. They made him hide behind trees or anything else they could find. They cursed him because he would always scare away all of the gazelles, and everyone went hungry because of him.

The other lion's tan fur blended in perfectly with the tall golden grass, but the gazelles always spotted his rainbow coat from a mile away. Even the hyenas and wild dogs would snicker at him as he walked by. It wasn't easy being different but it sure was easy to be noticed.

All the lion wanted was to be like all the other lions. Every night in his dreams he had the thickest shimmering golden coat of fur from the very tip of his nose to the last strand of hair on his tail. His thick gold mane encircling and shining around his face like the rays of the sun. He was the head of his own pride. Proud and strong. Leading every hunt with a one hundred percent success rate. All were fed and he was loved by his pride and feared by the gazelles, hyenas, and wild dogs alike. But every morning he would awaken from his slumber to the putrid, bright colors of his fur burning his eyes.

"Enough!" the cub roared one morning after a particularly disheartening dream.

He jumped up from his sleep and started running as fast as he could. He ran and ran until the air had completely left his lungs. He ran until he had never seen this new world beneath his feet. He kept on running, and running, and running. His legs felt like Jell-O and his heart beat like an abused drum, yet he carried on. Tears rolled down his rainbow cheeks as he finally stopped under a large dead baobab tree. Unable to take another step he laid his colorful head down on his sore front paws and decided to just lay there and never move again. Given up all hope at being normal this would be his end. His paws wet from his tears he started to drift away.

Sunrise and sunset came and went. He lost track of how many he saw, yet the lion did not move and he could feel the end approaching. Just as his rainbow eyes became too heavy to hold open any longer he saw a shimmer of light from high up in the sky. Unsure what he was seeing the curiosity lifted his eyes one last time.

Coming down from the clouds was a giant black bird. Big enough to block out the very sun lighting up the world. All over its body were twinkling white bright spots in between the blackness of the feathers. In the middle of its chest was a swirling purple and white spiral. Rotating in an endless loop. The massive bird landed on the biggest branch of the old dead tree above the lion's head, kicking up dirt and dust from the downdraft of its massive wings as he did so.

"Are you ready? It is time!" boomed out the bird in a deep and mysterious voice.

"Ready for what? Who, or... what, are you?" softly replied the lion, too weak to show enthusiasm.

"I am the Starbird and I am not here to tell you what I am. I am here to show you what *you* are. Now arise and follow me."

"I can't walk, my paws are too sore." said the lion in his quiet defeated voice as he laid his head back down.

The Starbird's chest mark emitted a soft purple light as he let out a squawk. "Why walk when you can fly?"

In that instant the lion lifted off the ground as the Starbird took to the sky in front of him. His very own flapping Starbird wings protruding out the top of his back carried him up and up, all the way into the clouds. His legs dangled and he started to paddle like he was swimming down a river. The wind rushed through the lion's fur and he could feel the pain leaving a trail behind him as it was washed away. A rare smile from ear to ear appeared on his face. He folded in his wings and swan dove down and swiftly pulled back up again. He did several loops around the Starbird, having fun in his one-man aerial show.

"That's quite enough," said the somewhat annoyed Starbird through a halfway closed beak. The lion's wings grew a mind of their own and began to fly him in perfect sync next to the giant Starbird.

After a few minutes of blissful flying the lion looked over to the Starbird and asked, "Sooooo, where are we going?"

"The better question is *when* are we going," replied the Starbird. "We are going back to the day you ran away."

"Nooooo! Please, I don't wanna go back. I like it up here with you. No one can see me and tell me to get back or to 'go hide'," the lion said in a deep raspy voice mocking his father's. "No one laughs at me because of my stupid fur either."

The Starbird let out a deep sigh. "My son, you started painting a picture, but have spilt the colors all over yourself before the real story could reach the canvas. You focused so hard on a single twig when there was an entire forest right in front of you."

"Huh?" the lion blurted out after a small pause as he tilted his head and crinkled up his nose giving the Starbird the most confused look he had ever seen.

The Starbird rolled his eyes "Here, let me show you." He then inhaled a long and drawn out breath of air and spewed it out while moving his beak in a circular motion. It created such a powerful wind it made all the clouds in front of them vanish.

"Look down now, what do you see?" the Starbird asked as they stopped flying and began to hover in place with their wings still flapping in unison.

The lion peered down and could see himself. Even from all the way up past where the clouds used to be it was impossible not to see his rainbow stripes.

The lion finally replied, "I see my family leaving on a hunt without me, like always. Making me hide cuz they are so ashamed of me. They always wanted me out of sight. I bet they wouldn't even care if I ever stopped hiding or not and they never found me again."

"My boy," said the Starbird. "I think you need a closer look."

Again, a light emitted from the spiral chest mark of the Starbird as he let out another thunderous squawk. The light this time though was so bright the lion had to close and shield his eyes with his leg as the entire sky turned a perfect flash of white. When he opened them again they were standing on the ground below. The lion's parents were meters away walking right towards them.

"Mom! Dad! Look at my awesome new wings!" The lion called out as he took a small step forward. "Maybe I can fly around and strike from the sky on hunts now with you guys." Gazing with big hopeful eyes at his parents as he said it.

Before the lion could advance any further the Starbird held out his enormous wing in front of the lion to intervene.

"I thought this would go without saying but they can't see or hear you. Well, this version of you anyway. Now pay attention."

The Starbird retracted his wing and the lion could now see his mother and father approaching closely and could start to make out their conversation.

"You know how much I hate leaving him alone like this." said the lion's mother as she turned her head to look at his father while they continued to walk.

The lion's father nodded in agreement while looking at the ground in front of his rugged worn paws.

"You know I don't like it either, but what other choice do we have? How else would we be able to provide food for him? What kind of parents would we be if we let our boy starve? One day I hope we can find a way to involve him in the hunts but this will just have to do for now. One day he will realize we make him hide now, so that we can continue to always find him later... For the rest of our days."

And with those words the lion's parents dissipated into a wispy cloud of dust and drifted off in the breeze right as they were approaching the two eavesdroppers.

"You see my boy", said the Starbird. "They only wanted what was best for you. Not making you hide out of shame, but out of love."

The lion took a second to gather his puzzled thoughts.

"Okay, well everyone else still laughs at me like my fur is soooo hilarious."

The lion let out a laugh exaggeratingly imitating the laughs he heard from the hyenas and the wild dogs.

"Pfft. Forest not the twig, forest not the twig..." The Stardbird muttered quietly under his breath as the dim purple light shined out of his chest mark yet again. He began to pull an invisible rope with one wing at a time. A game of tug-of-war against no one. This act pulled and spun the entire world around them as they stayed floating stationary. The blurred spinning environment came to a halt as the Starbird let go of the imaginary rope.

The lion could now see his former self walking past the hyenas and wild dogs as they snickered and smiled at him. But, now from this new view he could see three beautiful young lionesses from his pride tailing right behind him. They seemed to be fighting for position as to who could follow the closest behind him.

"No, I want him. His coat is soooo adorable." said one of the lionesses as she pushed her way to the front of the line.

"Nut uh, me." said another as she did the same back.

"He's gonna pick me anyway, I'm the prettiest one." said the one in the back of the line.

"Now do you see?" asked the Starbird.

"No one was laughing at you. More so at your sweet ignorance of the... shall I say, 'female conga line' forming behind you. Too deafened by the laughs to hear the real story screaming at you. If you would have just accepted yourself the way you are you wouldn't have been oblivious to the fact that everyone else always did.

The only person you were running away from that day was... yourself. Just because you had some colorful paint spill on you in all the wrong places doesn't mean you're not still a truly beautiful work of art. Embrace your world of color and you might start to see everything was black and white all along.

"But you can't see anything though until you wake up. Wake up. Wake up!"

The Starbirds deep booming voice slowly morphed into a much more familiar, normal sounding one as the lion pattered open his eyes. Standing over him a member of his pride stared down at him lit only by the light of the moon.

"Hey! Wake up!" yelled the lion from the pride as he tapped him on the head.

"Everyone has been searching for you for days. Your parents are worried sick. I don't think they've slept at all, always out looking for you. C'mon buddy get that cute lil rainbow butt up. Let's get you home where you belong."

The colorful cub looked up into the night sky from under the baobab tree as he gingerly got to his feet. Between the twinkling of the countless stars he squinted to make out the familiar soft purple light and the swirling spiral far off into the deep blackness of the sky.

"Yeah, let's go home," said the lion as he let out a small crooked smile.

{~The Mountain~}

Greatness can brew complacency.

When you're at the top
you can forget you still have to look up.

Someone could be dropping in from above
about to send you tumbling down the mountain.

The rest are clawing desperately at your ankles
trying to pull you down.

But the peak never stops rising.
There is no real summit.
The eternal climb.

Those who realize that
are the ones riding the wave upwards.

The ones who live in castles made of stone
on the highest step of the forever
upward growing escalator.

Course what the hell do I know?

I've never been anywhere near the clouds.

{~The Pillow~}

*I wonder what I had for breakfast this exact day 6 years
ago?*

I don't know, probably just cereal.
Too lazy to make eggs or something like that.
*Do I even like eggs? Yeah, I think I do. Not bad. In a
tortilla with hot sauce. Hell yeah.*

Ok, ok, shush.

...
...

*Why did Hitler shave his mustache like that? I'm sure it
was for some stupid logic of his.*
Shut the f**k up why am I even thinking about that?
Oh yeah, I watched a WW2 documentary yesterday.
*Man, I would s**t my pants with the first bullet that
came whizzing past my head.*
I can't even imagine.

Ok. Enough. Shh, shh.

...

...

I can hear my breathing and it's bothering me.

...

...

Why do we even have to breathe in this invisible thing called air?
What does it even do for our body? I don't get it.

...

...

I should probably get up and pee.
I just went 20 minutes ago, I'm fine.
How does our body know to not piss on ourselves while we're asleep?
Why so many questions about the body?
Apparently, I don't know s**t about how it works.
Did they ever teach us that in school?
Why don't we piss ourselves in our sleep?
I doubt they did.
There's no way.
Naaa.

Maybe.

OK! who cares right now. I've got to be up in 4 hours.

...

...

Can you get a college scholarship for playing the harmonica?
Like, is there a harmonica player in the band at college football games?
Lemme look that up real quick or it's gonna bug me.
No, yeah no. Doesn't matter. Now shut up!

...

...

I wonder if it's possible to scream loud enough in my head for other people to hear it.
Like, I'm laying here talking to myself and I can hear me.
But is there a way to have your thoughts recorded and heard for other people to hear without actually saying anything. Only by thinking it.
I'm sure technology will get there one day.
With like a chip implanted in your brain or something.

They need a pillow that turns your brain off as soon as you lay your head down on it.
So I wouldn't have to go through this s**t every night.

...
...

I should just get up and start typing and see what comes out.
Yeah... f**k it.

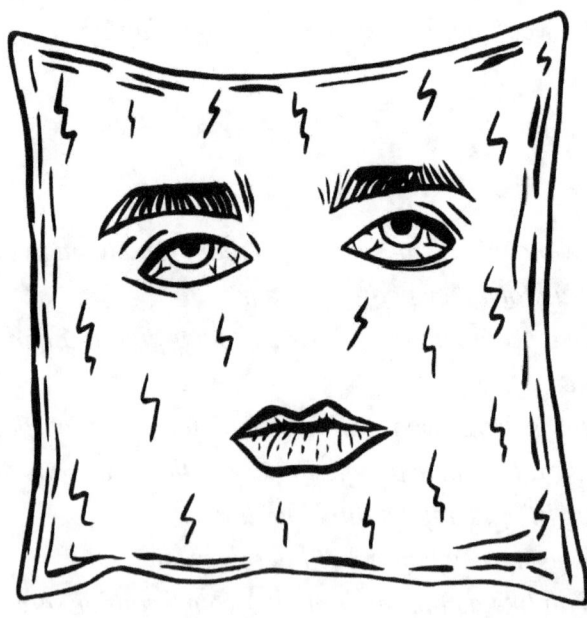

{~The Mother~}

We take, and we take, and we take, and we take. What do we give in return? Nothing but a putrid foulness infecting our home. No mother should be treated by her children this way.

Your hair was once a lush, intense evergreen, but it has been cut away inch by inch and your scalp dyed a dull hardened grey for us to drive all over. For us to lay the foundations and walls to our buildings kissing you gently on the top of your bald head. Inside these immense mazes of grey, we plot to fill our already overflowing pockets even more.

We are coming for you mother. It's okay though mother, calm down and breathe. Let the smoke from our pipes fill your lungs and blot out the sun. Let us use our silver tongues to deceive our siblings; the ones that actually care about you, so that we may carve up your face with our tools to claim the golden rocks under your skin. The shinier the better. We are still primitive that way.

Your enormous piercing blue eyes used to radiate the waves of your soul. We have made them stagnant. The waves get smaller and smaller as they crash into islands of wading plastic stretching from eyelid to eyelid.

Why did we do this to you? We treat you like our enemy when all you've ever done is nourish us and provide us the conditions for our very lives themselves. Yet we curse you for it.

You're getting old mother. You have been around for eons yet immediately after you gave birth to us, we invaded you. We took advantage of you mere seconds into our existence. We are not your children. No child would do such a thing to such an amazing mother. We are parasites eating your organs from the inside out. We are your cancer. Growing... Festering... Destroying...

{~The Object~}

they told me don't write a story
without a clear objective

but that's the main problem with life
there is no f**king objective

not really

just try not to be f**king miserable all the time
and that's it

in your own story you are both the protagonist
and your own worst antagonist

*no one f**ks you over more than you*

so, I guess the best advice I can give to myself
and anyone unfortunate enough to be reading this is

if you find something that makes you actually want to
wake up and see another day

don't sleep in

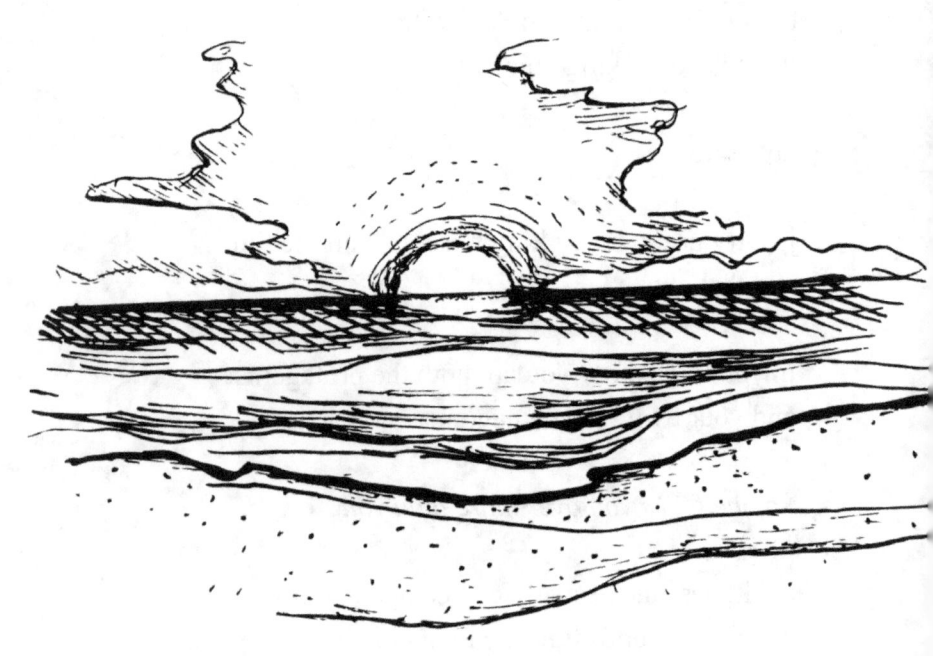

{~The Wolf~}

if all your good deeds come with the stipulation that a
camera has to be rolling

you're not doing it because you actually care
you're doing it to make yourself feel good
you can't wait to post it
so everyone can tell you how awesome you are

in the age of the constant need for another dopamine hit
what's better than getting tons of praise
for helping out some poor schmuck
who has it worse off than you do

of course, you don't see it this way
you genuinely think you're being a great person

last time I checked
taking advantage of someone's rough situation
and parading it down main street
for everyone to see

just to advance your own personal
status
agenda
and wealth
doesn't make you a saint

it makes you a wolf in sheep's clothing

{~The Brain~}

Without the advanced human brain
the profoundness of everything
would presumably be understood by nothing
and no one.

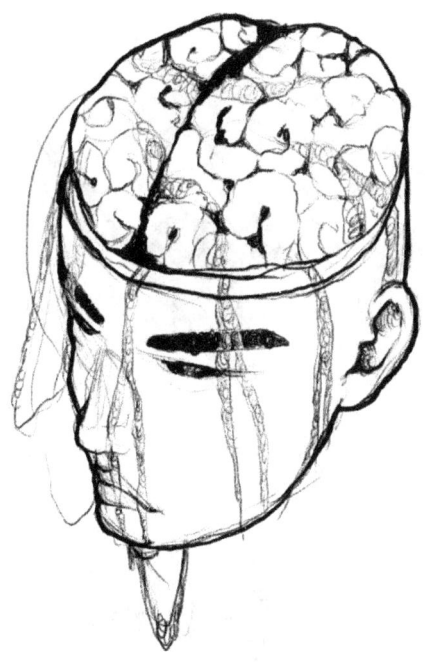

{~The Tongue~}

I hate that I never listen to my own advice
Not because I don't think it to be right
But because there is always another excuse in the queue
on the runway ready to fly off my tongue
My very own words
condemning me to destructive hypocrisy

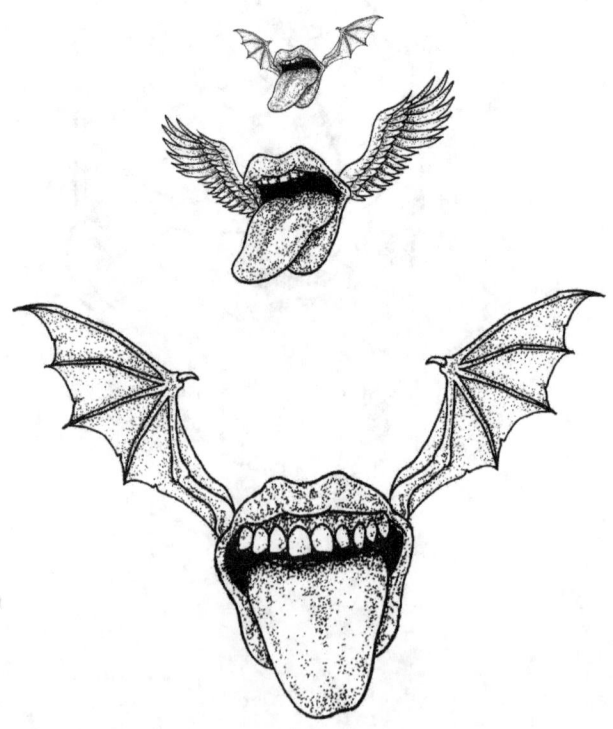

{~The Map~}

"Father, let me come with you, please," little Grace O'Malley said as she brushed her long fiery red hair out of her eyes. She charged after her father and wrapped her arms and legs around his deteriorating pant leg like a monkey clinging to a tree branch as he walked towards the door. The sheathed cutlass blade hanging from his waist belt tapped her in the face as she did so. He dragged his leg behind him under her weight. His foot thumped over each warped wooden plank of the floor until finally giving in.

"Alright, alright, little one. Enough now."

He easily plucked her off his leg, the hard life at sea kept him in impeccable shape. He knelt down on one knee so his matching blue eyes were level with hers.

"We go through this every time lassie. What kind of father would I be if I took a little girl out on a dangerous voyage at sea? Hm?"

Her face went stiff and her lips pouted. "It's not fair you always take Donal."

"That's because your brother is much older than you and able to fend for himself if need be. The worst he'll get is either a swift death or thrown overboard. With you… lord knows what crazed men at sea are capable of, having not laid eyes on a woman in months."

Her father reached into his shirt pocket and pulled out a worn folded piece of cloth paper and unfolded it revealing a map of sorts. It was unlike any she had seen in any of her father's books and charts that she liked to read when he was away.

"You see this," he pointed to a red X that was over a very unassuming island in the middle of the sea.

"When I find this, there will be no more voyages. No more having to fight, claw, and plunder just to bring back scraps for the family. You won't have to be like me…"

After a moment of intense staring into her eyes he carefully tucked away the map back into his pocket and got to his feet.

"So, what do the O'Malley's always say little one?"

Grace took a second and sensing the writing on the wall that her father was yet again not going to bring her along, she reluctantly recited the line.

"We need what they have and they have what we need, so if we have to we'll make 'em bleed."

Her father shook his head. "No, no. I told you that was your grandfather's and all the O'Malleys before him's creed. What do we say now?"

"But, I like the old one better father."

"What do we say now?" he repeated.

"Terra Marique Putens, Valiant by Sea and Land," Grace replied as her head sank down.

"Good lassie," her father said as he turned and opened the door. He stopped halfway out and swiveled his head around to say one last thing.

"You'll be more than some washed up old pirate like me someday, I promise... Whenever I find this blasted X on the map."

***

Twenty years later

There was a loud bang at the door of the O'Malley house. It swung open and smashed to splinters against the interior wall. Mr. O'Malley jerked up from his slumber and reached for his mustektoon that he always had leaning on the wall beside his bed for very occasions such as this.

Through the dim moonlight shining in he could make out a silhouette menacingly standing still in the doorway.

"Wh-wh-who's there? Don't come any closer, I'll shoot." His voice much deeper and gravelier now.

There was no response. The silence made his ears ring, the years of loud guns and cannons going off had taken a toll on his ears.

The mysterious intruder held up their arm and a small puff of fire turned into a glowing lantern as they lit the oil. Now blinded by the fresh light on tired eyes he could only hear the slow thump of footsteps approaching him.

He steadied the gun in his hand. "Stop I'm warning you not one step clo---"

He stopped in his words as the intruder was at the foot of the bed and his now adjusted eyes could make out their face. Their hair matching the color of the flames in the lantern they were holding.

He lowered his gun and his eyes started to water. "Grace? Is that you? My god it's been what? Twenty years? I never thought I'd see my little girl ever again."

"I'm not a little girl anymore father," she snapped at him. "Christ what the hell happened to you?" she asked as she surveyed him up and down.

"Sword took this one off," Mr. O'Malley said as he glanced down to his non-existent left arm. "And a hungry shark had this one for breakfast." He pulled off the blanket covering his lower half revealing his left leg missing halfway up his thigh.

"Well then," she said, seemingly unfazed by the ordeal. "Seeing as you are half the man you used to be… quite literally… That should make this a lot easier."

What could she possibly want now, after all these years, in the middle of the night? And where did she even go? So many questions, but the feeling of getting any answers didn't seem likely.

She leaned in close and the fire in her eyes burned holes into his soul.

"Where's the map old man? And before you stammer and stutter around your words trying to think of lies, I already paid a visit to brother Donal. He assured me you still have it and that you never found the island."

"That old thing I lost that years ago---"

"Where is it!" she shouted. Saliva spewed from her mouth like a rabid dog and she stomped her foot in disgust.

His little girl was unrecognizable anymore. Who was this monster screaming in his face?

Mr. O'Malley struggled to fully sit up with his one remaining arm. He eventually rested with his back up against the headboard of the bed.

"I can't give it to you... Look at me. Is this what you want to become? Old and mutilated with nothing to show for it. I tried to save you from this before and I'm not going to suddenly stop now."

Grace let out a grunt and she started to slowly pace around the meager one room house. "You see father, that right there... That is why I left. I never needed your saving. I never needed you to tell me what I could and couldn't do. I never needed it and I never wanted it. And look, if I had stayed you would have broken your promise to me anyway. I would have become what I am regardless. Except probably less successful at it with you there constantly holding me back for 'my own good.' So, I'm going to ask you one last time. Where is the map?"

He looked intently at his daughter. He couldn't be the reason she spends the rest of her life on a fool's errand, most likely getting injured or killed in the process.

"I can't... I just can't..." he muttered out to her.

She walked over to his side and drew the flintlock pistol from her hip holster and placed the cold barrel against his wrinkled forehead. "It's too late father, I didn't just become you, I'm more you, than you ever were. I'm the captain of my own ship you know, with a crew and everything."

The barrel began to vibrate against his forehead as her hand began to tremble.

"I will tear this place apart and I will find what I'm looking for. And when I find that treasure, I will carry on the O'Malley name and make it mean something... Once last chance father. Tell me where it is."

His silence told her everything she needed to know. That he is prepared to go down with the ship. If only she could see his intentions were pure and doing this out of love not spite.

After a few moments Grace had seen enough. "Father, I went back to using the old family motto. Hopefully you can understand what must be done..." With tears rolling down her cheeks and shaking hands she recited the line.

"We need what they have and they have what we need, so if we have to we'll make 'em bleed."

Grace pulled her trigger finger back towards herself and a puff of smoke and the smell of gunpowder filled the air.

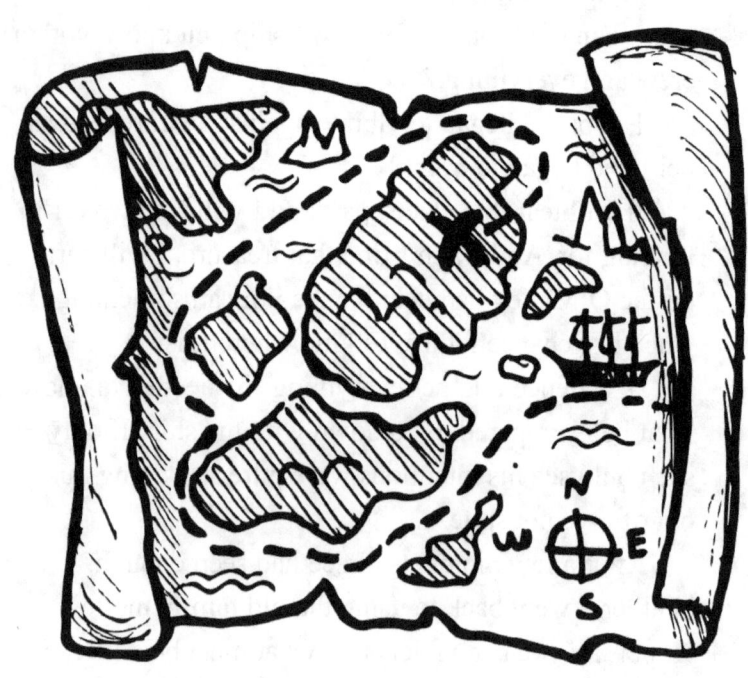

Chapter 2

{~Love~}

M. L. Johnson

{~The Door~}

she hated talk of small
but craved a love so big
destructively unaware that even the tallest trees
started as tiny seeds

she spent her whole life indoors
wondering when her adventure would arrive
yet she put headphones on and ignored the door
when it came knocking

{~The Anchor~}

Always the thing that held me in place;
grounded in the sand.
The immense pressure from the water surrounding
was never too heavy for your hand.

My bubble of air in the depths of the suffocating world.
My link to the surface;
never unfurled.

Counted on to stop me from crashing into the piercing
rocks.
Like giant jagged teeth they would appear from the
docks.

There you were,
digging and clawing to steer me in the right directions.
Without you, forever adrift;
lost in the vast glass reflections.

Hold me, hold me. It's where I want to be.
But wait, not so tight;
I can't breathe.

M. L. Johnson

I don't belong on this ocean floor.
Let me up; back to the shore.

I wasn't ready to stop exploring.
I've never been this deep.
When did life get so boring?

Which is up and what is down?
The chain locked around my ankle;
water rushing all around.

Trapped under the weight,
and stuck with no key.
Ears popping; lungs collapsing;
the emptiness consumes me.

So here we are with no boat left to row.
We learned to squeeze
but never learned to let go.

{~The Siren~}

Blatantly lurking and ever approaching.
Screaming at me; making their presence known.
The dog that never stops barking.
The train horn blaring its whistle.
They never stop coming.
One after the other, after the other, and another.
I can start to hear the familiar patter of the raindrops on
the shudders.
The breeze dragging the tips of the tree branches across
the windows like nails on a chalkboard.
The siren plays its deafening tone.

What did I do this time?
How long can we yell before our voices give out?

Lasting so long now they start to overlap.
I can't stop them anymore.
The windows have blown out and debris is pouring in.
The pileup is immense.
A car crash with the brake lines cut.

What did I do this time?
Don't take the kids to your mothers.

You said for better or for worse.
Well, I know I've been better
and I can't get much worse.
I guess there were only so many lamps to break
or walls to punch
before there was nothing left to call home.

Standing in this storm all alone now
with no place to go.
Nothing but black clouds from horizon to horizon.

I made a fort out of the
empty bottles.
Just a temporary,
imaginary shelter
from the howling wind
and the blistering rain.
A way to pretend to feel
the warmth of the sun
    while standing in the
        middle of a raging
            tornado.

{~The Cart~}

Her heart was so big
it was too heavy to just wear on her sleeve.
She had to pull it in a cart behind her.

A few of the men that crossed her path
would help her bare the weight.
They would join in and pull it alongside her...
for a while.
Until they realized the cart doors weren't locked
and they could just take her heart and leave.

Filling it with piles of filth on the way out.
Leaving her with just a foul stench.
And no reason to keep pulling.

But eventually she plugs her nose
and dries her eyes
and starts taking steps once more.

Each new step knocking off a layer of the piles, leaving
a healing trail behind her.

And out of the filth her heart starts to bloom
and fill the cart again.

Growing even more big and beautiful
than the one she knew before it.

-   To K.F.

{~The Starbird Rainbowlion Pt.2~}

When we first met you were a *star.*
The twinkle in my eye. Guiding me home through the darkest of nights. Granting my wishes, keeping me a hopeful dreamer. Now your light has burnt out. I try desperately to see you but you have blended in with the rest. You were once one in a million, but now you literally are one in a million and I can't find your light.

When we first met you were a *bird.*
I was entranced by your beautiful songs. The whistles guided me through the pitch-black caverns I always got lost in. Your bright, colorful feathers drew me in like a moth to a street light. Now your song wakes me up every morning like an alarm clock with no snooze button, and your feathers are falling out making a mess all over the floor. No longer a bird but a silent rodent scampering along in the sewers.

When we first met you were a *rainbow.*
Beauty incarnate and adored by all. I found the
shimmer of gold at your end. I stared in awe of how
lucky I must be. Now after all these years I've gone
colorblind. You are nothing more than a meaningless
arch between the clouds. A grey scale in a world filled
with colors.

When we first met you were a *lion.*
At the top of the food chain, tough and strong. Leaders
of prides. Your blood-stained mane after a kill showing
the world what you're capable of. Now your teeth and
claws have fallen out and gotten buried in the dirt.
Nothing more than a harmless kitty cat.

When we first met you were *hopelessly special.*
Now you are *especially hopeless.*

{~The Cliff~}

Love is like the wind
It will sweep you off your feet

They just don't tell you
That sometimes it's right off the edge of a cliff

{~The Book~}

We were always living in two separate worlds. Mine was fiction and yours was reality. My day was filled with moments but yours filled with minutes. I placed my hand in yours but could only feel the cold air; the warmth of your touch eluded me. All I ever wanted was to see what you see. To come down from atop my cloud and experience what the soil was like. Too lost in the story to ever learn to read but when you snapped shut the book; I felt it all the same.

I cried out tears of rain forming an ocean all around you. You paddled and paddled, treading water. But eventually your arms gave way and you sank like a stone to the bottom. I dove down to try and save you, frantically grasping, but you were long gone. Too deep, far away in the depths.

I could never give you what you wanted. The white fence, the barking dog, little Tommy and Jenna. That was my fiction; the unbelievable story. Not sure I was ever meant to be the protagonist in anyone's tale. Nor the villain either. More so the outside narrator looking in from afar. Watching everyone else live in their societally picture-perfect bubbles and knowing it was never my place to be. You wanted a book but I was only ever going to be a chapter. No happily ever after. Only a quick, *The End.*

***

It's been years now.

I still remember your face but know nothing anymore of your desires. None of your favorite things, and none of your dreams like you used to share with me in the mornings. Only an illusion of you. Not you at all anymore really. Just a random person in the picture in the frame. This stranger did once tell me though that it was okay that I lived in a faraway world as long as I got used to being its only inhabitant.

Here I am on the last page of my old book. Grey hairs of regret constant reminders of my mistake in the mirror. No love to be found all throughout besides our brief spark. And only one character still lurks in the pages.

The few paragraphs with you in them will always be my favorite but I always knew I needed to put the memory of you to bed. I tore out our page a long time ago. Countless times I held it over the fire contemplating erasing you from the record... but I never did like the smell of ashes.

You sip tea and smile as you browse through your entire library you created without me, while I sit here holding my lone page of us. *Fiction finally met reality.*

I don't want to die in your arms tonight.
I want to live in them forever.

{~The Movie~}

I spun you around as we danced in the rain.
Too bad you hate getting your hair wet.

We sat on the beach watching the incredible sunset.
All you could think about was all the sand we were
going to track back into the car.

I took you to that fancy restaurant you always
complained you never got to experience.
You filled up on bread and didn't even touch your meal.

I constructed a trail of rose petals to a bubble bath lit by
candlelight for our anniversary.
All you could say was, "These better not be from my
garden."

I made you breakfast in bed when you had surgery on
your knee.
When did you go vegan? Sorry I'll take it away.

I took you to the spot where we first met.
You sat on your phone barely looking up to
acknowledge it.

I tried to give you the movies but no story I could tell
would interest you enough to keep you in your seat any
longer.

The credits rolled on us a long time ago.

{~The Race~}

Lust is just a race to love.

Unfortunately, unless you both cross the finish line at the exact same time whoever finishes first is going to be the one hurt.

Stuck waiting on someone who might have dropped out a long time ago.

M. L. Johnson

{~The Lighthouse~}

the ship and the lighthouse
a partnership out of necessity
but when my light burnt out
we shattered and sank as you crashed into me
the pieces of us tried desperately to hold hands
on the way down
refusing to let go
But the current is swift and the ocean vast
separated forever by the
undertow

{~The Body~}

I offered up both my body, and my soul.
You only ever really wanted one of them.
But you pretended to crave them both for years.
I can't do this anymore.

-     every missed real connection I've ever had.

P.S. For what it's worth
I'm sorry

M. L. Johnson

{~The Mask~}

how could I not see
that you would break those promises so swiftly

yet you deceivingly pulled your way back into me;
gravity

you are the ocean
a desert disguised as water

the devil stealthily lurking in the ink blotter

{~The Air~}

I needed you to be my oxygen
but you were the hands wrapped around my throat
telling me to *just breathe*.

{~The Devil~}

I never said I could walk on water.
I never claimed to be the son of the father.

Yet when you proclaimed the devil took control of your lips.
And made you wrap them around all those d**ks.

I saw straight through the lies.
I saw it, I saw it in your eyes.

But your fabrications were somewhat true.
Because the devil, *the devil is you.*

{~The Heart~}

Like planting seeds in a plastic garden
Like ignoring the bright shining sun just hoping the
moon looks your way
Like finding a strand of hay in a stack of needles
Like lighting a candle in a raging wind
Like driving a car with all the tires flat
Like holding a once musical heart with no rhythm left
in its beats
Like breathing in water to fill your lungs
and drinking in air to quench your thirst

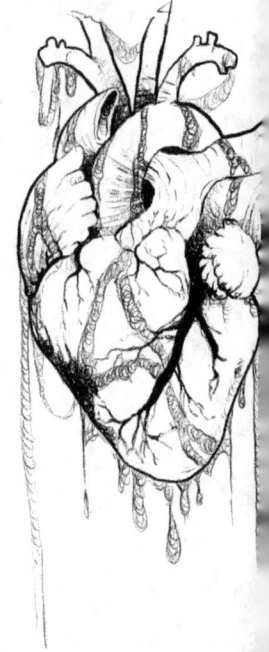

-    what loving me must feel like

Chapter 3

{~Delusion~}

A persistent belief or impression that is firmly maintained despite being contradicted by what is generally accepted as fact, reality, or rational argument, typically a symptom of mental disorder.

M. L. Johnson

{~The Cycle~}

The truth is the hardest thing to fathom.
Secrets beneath the surface,
things you couldn't imagine.
Everything you see is merely an illusion.
Forever trapped in the cycle,
a never ending delusion.

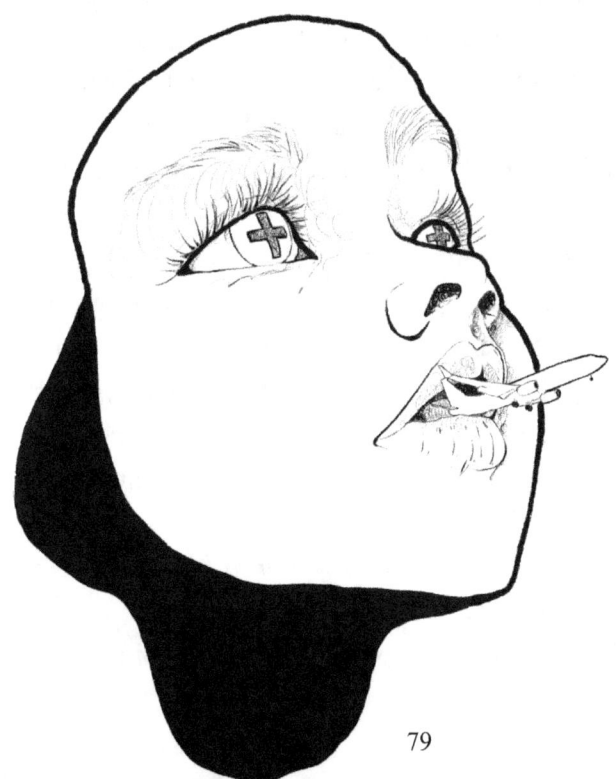

{~The Veil~}

A man with no questions is a man with no answers. And a man with no answers is a man lost in the dark, susceptible to any snake oil being rubbed in his eyes, to any hissings in his ears. You can't turn on the lights until you first figure out that you are indeed in the darkness. You cannot provide a solution until you realize there's a problem. You can't f**king wake up until the mattress is ablaze beneath you. Accepting everything at face value means you've been told whose face has value. An arranged marriage forced upon you of what's right and wrong, fact or fiction, life or death.

A man with no questions is a man not questioning everything. Not a man at all but a sheep in the field of perpetual darkness. The Nightwolf lingers; probing and searching for any sheep to hear his tales. To believe him when he says he's not here to eat you but to take you far away from this field. To a new one not encased in darkness but one with delicious green pastures and radiant bright shining skies.

A man with no questions is a man still believing in outdated moralities and plagiarized stories of nonsensical mythical beings. Cut off your f**king knees so they can't force you on them. Cut out your tongue so they can't make you mutter to the sky idiotic passages as if anyone is f**king listening. One, two, three, don't think just repeat after me. The lowercase t is so heavy weighing you down. Dragging it behind you so deep into the sand just as the superstitious, barbaric desert tribes left it. Logic and critical thinking, even common sense are the strings to pull the weight off your shoulders. Just because we don't have all the answers doesn't mean we have to cling to an ancient one. No one really knows where we came from or where we are going and we are crippled by the fear of not knowing. Too scared of the unknown, to accept we just might be alone.

A man with no questions is a man with a veil covered mind. Seek dissolution from the lies and it'll be just like it's your wedding night. Pull back the veil and kiss your sweet ignorance goodbye.

{~The Mirror~}

You were a mountain top, but now the earth has shifted and you've fallen back into the sea.

You were a rare unicorn, but now your horn has fallen off and gotten buried in the dirt. Now nothing more than a common white horse.

You were a field full of roses, but now all of your petals have wilted and died.
"I hate that you're the only one who truly knows me. Who can truly see behind the mask."

You were a beach side sunset, but now you are the black storm clouds blocking out the rays.

You were a raging bonfire, but now you are the pile of ash. The constant reminder of what used to be.

You were a toppling waterfall, but now the river has run dry. Nothing more than piles of dull grey rocks.
"Do you ever stop? Can I ever get a break from your persistent degradement?"

You were a butterfly, but now your wings are clipped
and you're flailing on the ground.

You were a thick layer of winter snow, but now it's
always summer and your melting away into nothi---
"Alright already, I get it!"

"Do you though!? Do you really? You can say that to
me all you want, it's everyone else that needs to hear it,
to see it, to believe it!"

You were a son,
but now you're a f**king thief
and a liar!

You were a father, but now
you're a stranger that mommy
tells to "quit calling!"

You were a man, but now
you're a hideous creature
lurking in the dark.
Run away! Everyone run away!
*"I can't stand you, get out of my
sight... I'll find a way to silence the reflections."*

{~The Cage~}

Every day that we get further from god is another day we get closer to finding ourselves.

Another step towards freedom from the invisible cage that we've locked ourselves in for all these years.

If seeing is believing, then I must be completely blind.

M. L. Johnson

{~The Crown~}

You are blind we'll help you see
  We'll cleanse your soul for a fee
Just like us you will be
  Submit to us we'll set you free

We'll sail your worries out to sea
  No thoughts needed just kneel for thee
You'll feel much better don't you agree
  Submit to us we'll set you free

We'll keep you in with lock and key
  And say your words are blasphemy
We'll tell you what you ought to be
  Submit to us we'll set you free

Fear our words and bring our tea
  Hello do you f**king hear me
Obey your masters bend the knee
  Submit to us we'll set you free

Submit to us we'll count to three
    Submit to us you worthless flea
Submit to us or hang from the tree
    Submit to us we'll set you free

SUBMIT TO US
WE'LL SET YOU
FREE

{~The Book Pt.2~}

"Context!" they shout about anything that doesn't make sense how it could be god's actual words written in their texts.

Yet they refuse to put their entire book into context. Who wrote it, when they wrote it, where they wrote it, why they wrote it, and what other books came before it.

Do those things and use simple deductive reasoning skills and it all starts to make sense. Their book is just that. A book.

{~The Shadow~}

I can feel their warm breath
constantly running down my neck

Always there, unseen, hovering over my shoulder
I finally decided to switch off the light
to draw them out
and face them head on

But when they circled round
and tried to whisper in my ear
Their numbers were so great the voices overlapped

"Take turns"
I said through the darkness
But that would have taken ten lifetimes
The whispers gradually turned to mutters
as they talked over each other

"Please let's talk this through" I begged
My words couldn't be heard
as the mutters turned to shouting

I tried to back away
to run away
but the horde of them sprinted after me

The shouting turned into blaring deafness
I shielded my ears and stumbled over all the empty
bottles on the way to flip the light back on
All went silent again as they scurried away like
cockroaches when the light switched on

Still there always lurking, stalking me, as I do my best
to pretend they don't exist
Sometimes I wish they would just take me
Consume me

I'm so tired of living in fear
of my own shadow.

{~The Mirror Pt.2~}

I'm not scared of the person looking back at me in the mirror.

I'm terrified because no one's there.

{~The Coin~}

I placed the map in your hand yet you never could find the right destination. Every turn there was more unfamiliar scenery passing you by out the window. I circled where home was and traced out the route for you, but I guess what you were searching for wasn't on the pages.

I placed the coin in your hand yet you did not flip it. Fifty-fifty chance became zero percent chance. If you don't play the game you can't win, and not playing at all is worse than losing. At least with one you can say you tried even if the coin doesn't land in your favor. Instead of taking the risk you just kept the coin and slid it into your pocket. Just added weight weighing you down as you slowly waste away. The grass will never be greener if you are choosing to live in black and white.

{~The Flame~}

I would ask my mother why an all-powerful, loving God would send people to hell to burn in fire and agony for eternity. She would reply that she thinks that version of hell is more of a metaphor. That hell isn't actual fire and brimstone rather just an eternal separation from God. You die and have no afterlife, while the believers get to live on in God's presence forever.

Well what if I'm just fine with no longer living anymore? If I die and just simply don't exist at all anymore then wouldn't it stand to reason that I wouldn't know I ever existed in the first place? I would have no idea that I'm missing out on anything at all. Doesn't seem like much of a punishment at that point.

If all life is, is a test to see where you spend your afterlife it kind of diminishes the time spent here on earth. Play nice and believe that Jesus killed himself for us then your all set, ready to go.

That's it.

Do that and hang around for eighty or so years waiting to die because nothing else matters in this quick pit stop to eternity. The party doesn't start until your pulse stops. And that's the basic fundamental message

of Christianity in its most stripped-down form. How
that inspires millions I'll never understand. Or, maybe
because it is that simple to grasp is why it sucks in and
devours so many narrow minds from all walks of life.

You are believing in something you can't see,
making the things you can, mean nothing.

Then you gotta ask, can you really feel alive in an
existence(heaven) where death is no longer an option
on the table? Without contrast nothing is special. If
everything is special, nothing is special.

You can't appreciate happiness if there is no sadness
to remind you of the meaning behind smiles. The sun is
more beautiful and comforting shining through rain
clouds after a thunderstorm. If the sun was always
present your skin would burn and blister and your eyes
would go dark from overexposure.

Even with all of that being said, I hope I go to hell when I die because that means everyone I love was right and is going to or already is living in blissful euphoria forever and ever. It sucks for me, but at least I'll take some solace knowing they are all in paradise.

It might just make the flames burn a little less hot and my screams a little more muffled.

{~The Puppy~}

My mother and I would also argue about God supposedly giving us free will. With an omniscient, omnipotent, omnipresent, and omnibenevolent God there can be no such thing as free will. Despite what my mother would argue.

"God doesn't send you to hell. Your actions put you there." she would say.

Well if God already knew every thought, feeling, and action I was ever going to have and take on earth before he even created me. And he knew those thoughts, feelings, and actions were going to purchase me a ticket straight to hell. Then he created me with the sole purpose of sending me to hell. Nothing I could have said or done was going to change that fact before I was even born and he already knew that. So, where's the free will there? He is the puppet master but we are not even the puppet. The entire world is his puppet. We are just the strings he ties to the wooden handles to make his toy dance for him.

It's like going to an animal
shelter and picking out a puppy.
And on this puppies cage it reads,
   "If you take this puppy home with you today, in
four years on this exact day at exactly 1:37P.M. this dog
will get hit by a car and die. Don't take this animal
home today and nothing bad will ever happen to it."
   So naturally, you take the puppy home that day.
And in four years on the exact date and time the note on
the cage read, you sit on your front porch and you
watch the dog run right past you into the street. It gets
hit by a car and dies. Was it the dogs free will to get hit
by that car or was its fate already decided for it by you
back at the shelter?

Also, it's not free will if in the end there is only one right choice. You can do whatever you want, make any choice you desire. But, if you don't choose the one God wants you to, you will suffer in agony for eternity.

God would say, "Hey, you can do whatever you want my child but just make sure what you do is exactly what I want you to do or you will be punished forever for it."

What kind of mobster *I'm not saying, I'm just saying* type deal is that?

No being worthy of worship demands it

{~The Tower~}

I think we're having our new Pearl Harbor.
They sit back and laugh; like lambs to the slaughter.
If anyone questions who is to blame.
Scoff and mock; they must be insane.
The trail to the truth isn't made of yellow bricks.
Only green paper with faces etched in it.
Debt magically gone; blown away in the dust.
We are your overlords; in us you must trust.
Several trillion reasons the rubble was piled.
Behind closed doors they high fived and smiled.
So many unbelievable coincidences in one day.
Almost a miracle it played out that way.
Physics and science are asked to be discarded.
Why the hell was their report not shot down and
bombarded?
Completely left out; the tower numbered seven.
Small office fires aren't enough to implode it from the
heavens.
Never happened before and never will again.
Doesn't matter sheep; get back in your pen.

Free fall speed achieved three times in a row.
Solid passing straight through solid; I guess I missed
that memo.

Rivers of molten metal flowing months after the
devastation.
Natural elements; cannot be the causation.
I could author a list of examples of the deception.
But it will never be the accepted perception.

The truth will forever be hidden in the dark.
No deathbed confessions; always circled by sharks.
America the brave, and land of you're free to die.
Long as the war machine keeps pumping,
they will turn a blind eye.
Helpless and shattered; no way to seek absolution.
It would take an entire country's mass revolution.
I would say stand up and fight for the factuality.
But it's obvious the people are complacent in their false
reality.

{~The Cell~}

The only place you are ever truly one hundred percent alone in this world is in your own head and it's terrifying. It's the industrial factory for your unsettling emotions and thoughts. Then those feelings brew together to create the bed that all your monsters live under. A tiny room with no doors and no windows. No one can join you in there. Ever.

Even if you have absolutely zero friends or family you can walk down the street or to the local bar and find someone to talk to and make a connection with. But no matter how hard you try. No matter how many gods you make up or imaginary friends you imaginatively invent. There is no one and never will be anyone in your head but you.

It's why one of the defining characteristics of being considered crazy, mad, or insane is hearing voices in your head other than your own. Trying to break the unbreakable mold of loneness. It can't be done. *We are all alone, together.*

It's a baron wasteland in there. A vast ever stretching desert in all directions with no oasis. Your screams echo off the grains of sand into the bright empty sky with no ears around to hear them. Your tears evaporate off your cheeks before ever hitting the ground.

The skull around your thoughts becomes an ivory prison. That is until your brain flips its switch to the *off* position.

You scratch and claw away at the bone but it's just too thick. The only escape route is into an eternity of blackness, into nothingness. But that's no great escape. That's just digging into another cell that has the lights turned off.

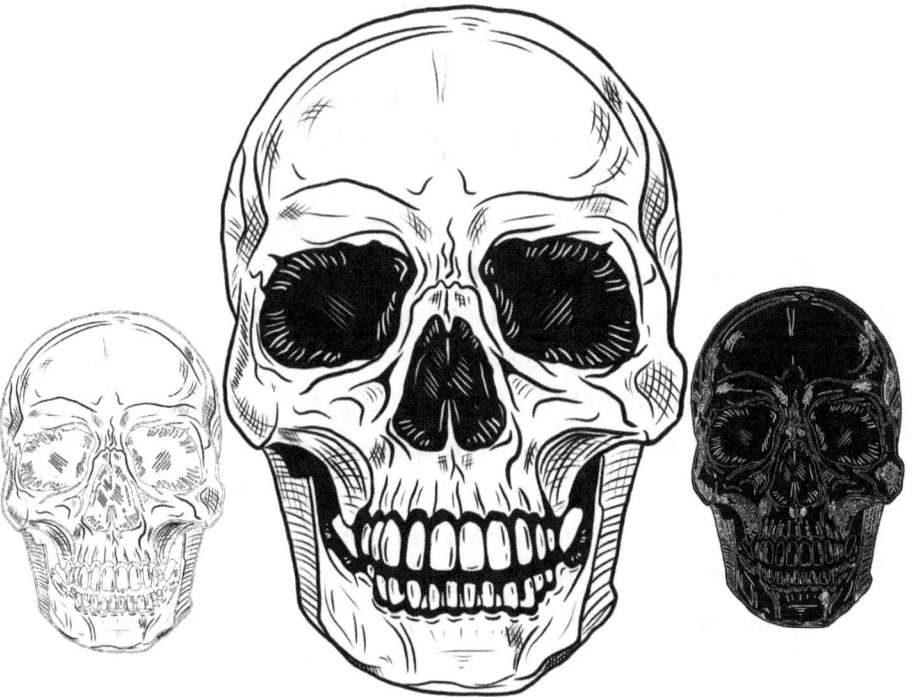

{~The Blanket~}

This entry comes with a few stipulations.
I set two rules for myself.

Rule 1: No prior thinking or planning whatsoever of
what I was going to write. Just start typing and
whatever happens, happens. The thoughts must form as
each new word reaches the paper.

Rule 2: As soon as I stop typing the endeavor is over.
Finished, that's the end. Not allowed to stop at all to
think it through.

Here is the raw, mostly unedited version of this
experiment. Only changes made were turning some text
into italic to make it somewhat comprehensible. But no
spell check, nothing. Just the frantic typing to keep the
story rolling. There will be spelling and grammatical
errors and things might not make sense or even be
anywhere near as coherent as I would like them to be
otherwise. Free flowing thoughts coming from pure
instant intuition.

I scared myself with this one. Can't believe these would be the thoughts to immediately spew from the bowels of my brain without any warning.

***

You're running at full speed through a dark forest. The soft glow of moonlight dimly lighting the branches up ahead as they narrowly miss slapping against your face. Running from what? Who or what is coming through the trees after you?

Run, don't stop. Faster. Faster...

"Snap!" a loud echo is heard throughout the night as you buckle and fall to the ground onto your side. You immediately feel a wave of pain rushing up your leg. You glance down to see your foot caught in a bear trap and it's clamped around your ankle. The snapping sound you now believe wasn't from the trap but from the bones in your ankle shattering and turning to shards inside your body.

From the direction which you came running the wind howls at you . The leaves rustle and shake violently.

It's coming.

What the f***k is happening?

You try with every ounce of strenthg to pry open the metal clinched tight around your ankle. It wont budge.

Quick cut off your foot, youve got to get out of here. Do it! Don't think, just do it!

What the fu***k is going on?!

"Help!" you scream, "help me!" The only reply you receive is from the wolves sympathetically howling into the night. The owls screech. The coyotes yap. You have become one of them. Just another wounded animal lost in the vast dark ocean of trees.

The wind picks up and starts to blow even harder. The immense volume from the rustling leaves and branches clashing together grows louder and louder. You cant think over the thundering noise.

"Help!" you cry out again in a painful tone as tears roll down your cheeks.

"Please somone, anyone, f**cking help!" but your screams are corked in a bottle and thrown out to sea never to be heard.

Just do it. Cut off your f**cking foot! Its almost here!

"Help," you mutter out in a defeated voice to where only a faint whisper can be heard. This must be the end. All your hope and all your dreams are floating away. Concealed amidst the leaves in the wind.

The swirling wind starts to spin the entire earth around you. The dizziness takes over and you cant focus your eyes on a stationary point any longer. Head spinning round and round as the branches detach and fall all around you from up above. Covering you. Blanketing you.

Sleep now. You've run so far you must be tired. Rest your head to make the pain go away.

Shhh, it's okay. It'll all be okay.

{~The Face~}

I'd rather have two faces,
Than one empty blank one.
That is until they started talking to each other.
Nothing worse than lying to yourself,
right to your own face.

{~The Cage Pt.2~}

They sweep across the world.
Their hunger is insatiable.
Devouring everything in sight,
taking what isn't rightfully theirs.

The ever growing divide,
drawing the line deeper and deeper into the sand.
Sides will have to be taken
and it will be us versus them in the end.
But they have siphoned all the water,
and harvested all the crops,
and stored them away in their vaults.
They want us dependent on them.
Unable to function without their help.
Begging them
Please help us.
While distracted on our knees they slowly construct a
cage around us without us even noticing.
Each part of our lives we agree to surrender to them
is another bar welded to the frame.

It will be called for in the name of humanity.
But that's just white noise
while they slip on the blindfold.

They will dangle pieces of meat in our faces and just
like starving lions we'll rip and claw at each other just
for a tiny bite of their generous handouts.

We will bathe in rivers of blood and tears.

While they bathe in rivers of gold.

{~The Window~}

Stop waiting around for your ridiculous posthumous promises or your horrifying divine damnations. You don't need to mumble any hail marys' or beg for salvation.

How are we so arrogant to think that we are immortal in the first place? You just die, and that's it. Belief otherwise just diminishes everything you ever loved, achieved, or strived for while still six feet above the dirt.

Life is only precious because it is short. It is a tiny blip of time through the vast window of existence, with nothing after it. There is no destiny, no fate, no gods, and no purpose besides what you apply to it yourself.

I can't tell you the meaning of life because everyone's journey is different and some people's paths come to a dead end well before others. All I can say with certainty to improve the scenery along the way is;

before you die, make sure you're actually alive.

Chapter 4

{~Death~}

{~The Bridge~}

I walk across you every day
to get to my 8-hour prison sentence.
The water down below ripples and glides in the wind.
So beautiful,
so calm,
so... *inviting.*

Yet liquid becomes concrete from up here.
Should I become the children's chalk used to draw the
little hop-scotch game on the sidewalk?
"Not today," I tell the water down below.
"Not today..."

The next day is a bright, sunny,
picture perfect day on my walk across you.
The birds fly overhead singing me a radiant tune.
Would their song change tone on my way down?
Or would their melodic notes carry me away into the
clouds?
"Not today," I tell the birds up above.
"Not today..."

It sure is windy this time across you;
blowing my hair all about.
Recklessly tossing me around like a ragdoll.
The birds up above get smaller in the distance.
Their song becomes almost inaudible.
What little tune I can still hear makes me sick.
Get me away from it.
I cant f**king stand it.
From below, the rippling waves have come to say hello.
They reach up to place a gentle kiss on my cheek.
You are not keeping me held back all the way up there.
"Not today," I tell the bridge as I look back upon it.
"Not today---"

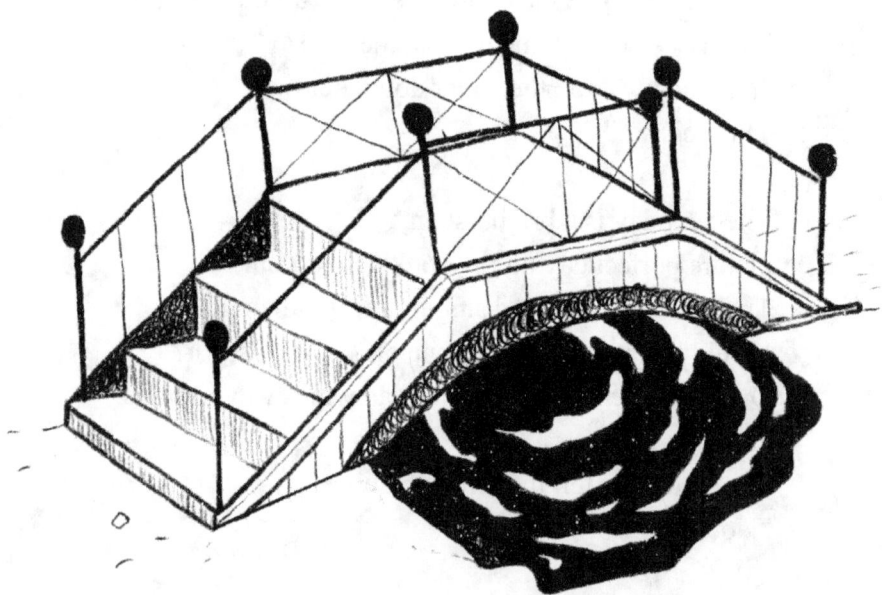

{~The Shovel~}

"Mr. Cronwell, do you believe that you are invisible?" asked Mr. Strauss as he paced back and forth in Cronwell's tiny one room rustic farmhouse. Cronwell sat leaned back in his chair with his boots up on the wooden table in the middle of the room. He stared down at his drink with his large billed hat covering most of his face, avoiding the gaze of Mr. Strauss.

"Judging by your lack of covertness during your devilish deeds," continued Strauss, "I would have to say that you think you are some sort of ghost, eyes seein' right through you. Do you think you are a ghost Mr. Cronwell? Nevermind, don't answer that, none the matter right now.

"I understand you felt safe hincin' it was on your own land, but curious wandering eyes can peer over little cattle fences. Eavesdroppin' ears can hear a feather land on a puddle in the mud. Whispers about what you done can spread faster than wildfire through drought ridden vegetation.

"What did you expect Mr. and Ms. Leeland to think when they heard the howls from your wife echoing out in the middle of the night. Those sweet old folks come running up to see you ferociously diggin' you a hole. Shirt off, sweatin', mutterin' to yourself. They swear by it they saw your eyes glowin' red like the embers of a smolderin' fire. You're lucky they came a knockin' at my door first. Poor folks were shakin' like they seen the devil himself. I gently reassured them that you are a good man and there must be some sort of logical explanation for all this and that I would come by today and clear up their misunderstanding.

"I'm here to help you Mr. Cronwell. As you know I am a very well fed, wealthy man, and have every means to get you the hell outta' dodge. It will damage my purse none at all. Here, take this first-class ticket for that new-fangled railroad. Goes all the way to Omaha it does."

Strauss pulled out a paper ticket from his jacket's inner breast pocket and slid it onto the table.

"Once you arrive in Omaha, I will have a 4-horse carriage waitin' there for ya' to take you as far east as east can get. Them horses will run straight into the Atlantic for ya' if'in you wish. Take this hefty sum of bills and build you a new life."

He then pulled out a stack of large bills from his other pocket and stacked them on top of the train ticket.

"Blend in with them eastern city folk," he continued. "Become a shadow in utter darkness. Become a---"

"Well hold on there partner. Can I get a word in here?" Cronwell finally interrupted as he lowered his feet and set down his cup onto the table. He tilted up the brim of his hat to get a better look at the man standing before him.

"This is a lot to take in. You accusing me of what? Killing my wife, Mr. Strauss?"

"Well, where is she," asked Strauss. "Have you seen her at all since you woke up this morning? Don't play ignorant, you know what you done."

Cronwell took a second and gave a thoughtful look.

"Well you were here last night having one of your business meetings with her about adding the fancy dresses she makes into your stores. Bring you in some women folk customers, alongside those what cha call um 'blue jeans?' for the men."

Strauss' face turned serious, almost shocked not expecting such a reply. "Well, I left shortly after you wandered off into the night. I guess our meetings are too much of a bore for you. You always do slip out and leave us be when we have our meetin's. Look here, Mr. and Ms. Leeland said they saw you with a bloody shovel while you was diggin' a hole. Put the pieces of the puzzle together Mr. Cronwell. The rope is already around your neck whether you can feel it or not. It don't matter what you did or did not do. It's what everyone thinks you done that'll put you up on that scaffolding.

The lever is already pulled and your limp body is already swayin' in the wind. Your wife is missing, neighbors heard her screams coming from right here inside your home, and saw you frantically digging with a bloody shovel. There is no more thinkin' on the matter Mr. Cronwell. The train leaves in half past the hour. I would strongly advise you to be one of its passengers."

Cronwell rubbed the bottom of his chin. "I do never tend to remember much of anything when you come to talk business with her. Must be that top dollar mighty fine whisky you always so graciously bring me. Say why is it that you never partake in the spirits with me? Sure is a dullard to drink alone."

"I don't indulge in the brown water while speakin' business. Gotta keep my wits about me. Keep the head as clear as possible." replied Strauss.

"Must be some mighty strong drink. I always seem to lose the whole night's memory when I drink it. Always waking up covered in dirt and sweat like I had joined the pigs out rollin' in the mud." said Cronwell.

"Why are you so concerned with drinking right now? Time is being wasted, you must head for the train station." insisted Strauss.

"Yeah... well... I guess you're right. Thank you kindly for the fancy ticket and the small fortune you've given me. I'll be on my way."

Cronwell stood up and stretched out his muscles. He then leaned over the table, grabbed the gifted items and stuffed them into his own pockets.

"I've got to get some ground between me and the vultures circling round overhead," Cronwell continued.

"But first, there's just one question I've got to ask. It's burning at me real deep. Ready to explode like a powder keg with a lit fuse..." Cronwell walked around the table to be nearly face to face with Strauss.

"Do you take me for a damn fool Mr. Strauss? Do I have clown makeup on? Juggling balls for your amusement?"

"I'm-I'm sorry I don't follow." frantically said Strauss as he took a small step backwards.

"Yes you do. My circus act is over and so is yours Mr. Strauss. If'in you're gonna hatch a plan in such poor regard at least do your due diligence first. Mr. And Ms. Leeland moved back east to Montgomery bout two months back I reckon. So even if I didn't already discover your silly indiscretions, that oversight would have given you away right there. I guess there is a difference between business smart and regular old cowboy smart.

"I had my suspicions from the very beginning about these so-called business meetings you were havin' with my wife. For starters; and pardon my bluntness, her dresses look like they were stitched by a simple-minded monkey with stumps for hands. Anybody with a least one good seein' eye can tell that much.

"I saw the way you looked at her. The only dress business you were interested in is how you can get her out of the one she was currently wearin'. But I went along with these meetin's. Call it foolish, call it greed. Blinded by the shimmer of light gleaming from the sacks of gold that were to come our way. Caught up in the idea of the life I could have rather than the one right in front of me."

"Now Mr. Cronwell I don't know what you are insinuating here but---" said Strauss with a tremble in his voice before Cronwell abruptly interrupted again, this time more loudly.

"Not one more g**damn word out of your fat f**kin' mouth or I will knock those pretty teeth down your throat and make you eat um for breakfast...

"Now, where was I? Oh yes, you see I just couldn't figure out why it was every time you would show up lurkin' around my home, eye f**kin' my wife that I would wake up the next mornin' covered in dirt and cow sh*t and god knows what else. With no recollection of what in the hell happened to me, just blurs of crazy dreams. Dancin' rainbows in the night sky. A giant coyote the size of an elephant scampering around makin' the ground tremble beneath me. And I swear I had a vivid and hilarious conversation with my horse Anabell. Funny girl, she's got some jokes on her... But I digress...

"So, what was it in the whisky Mr. Strauss? That injun peyote, some poppy seeds, or some crazy doctor snake juice you found? Don't matter, I didn't drink any of your poison drink last night. Whenever your tiny beady eyes would gaze elsewhere; mostly onto my wife's bosom, I would spit out what I had stored in my mouth. Onto the floor or in my lap or wherever was convenient.

"You see I pretended to stumble outside like I imagined I have done all the other times, and I did hear my wife screaming last night but it wasn't from me harmin' her. I came and peered inside the window and it was from your sweaty, flabby, and quite frankly grotesque, lumpy mound of a body penetrating her lady parts. In my very own bed nonetheless. Looked like a buffalo tryin to make relations with a cute little bunny rabbit. The poor girl... Those probably weren't screams of pleasure more so screams to keep her supper from going to waste on the floor.

"You okay Mr. Strauss? You're starting to sweat beads all over that pudgy face of yours."

Cronwell took steps towards Strauss and he matched them backwards until his back hit the wooden planks of the wall of the house.

Cronwells voice raised even more as he continued, "That was the plan then? Make me think I committed murder? To send me as far away as possible, from one ocean to the other.

"Where is my dearly beloved now? She over there at your ridiculously large estate waiting till you send me away? Ah, don't matter you can't take her with you where you're goin'.

"Are you scared Mr. Strauss? I see you shiftin' your eyes towards the door. You can try it. Your feral hog ass can waddle as fast as you can to try and run. You might make it out the door... Hell, might even make it down the steps of the porch, but you know damn well you ain't getting much farther than that Mr. Strauss so let's save the theatrics.

"You see there was one part of your story that was true." Cronwell grabbed Strauss by the front collar of his shirt and got so close to whisper in his ear.

"I did dig a hole last night... and it's for you... Good thing I have this train ticket and stack of money. I'm gonna need um after I put you in it."

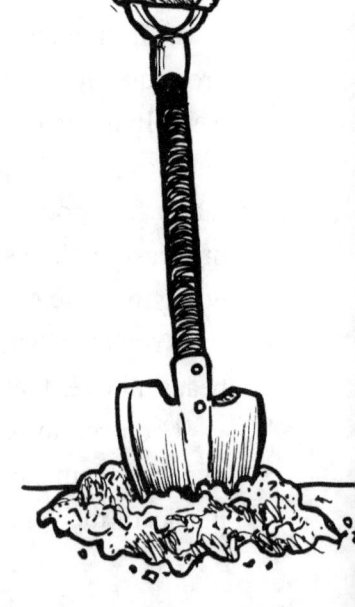

M. L. Johnson

{~The Map Pt.2~}

Have never climbed any mountains
nor made a wish in any fancy fountains

Have never explored any caves
nor surfed any gnarly waves

Have never scubaed any colorful fish
nor eaten some crazy dish

Ain't never been to Paris
to see my wife's parents

Ain't never been on a plane
to see the hills of Spain

Ain't never been to the Congo
to see the wild and play the bongo

Too weak to ride on a train
to run away from the pain

Too weak to go on a cruise
to sail away from the news

Too weak to fly
to even say goodbye

Will never see a man on Mars
because my battery has run out of bars

Will never see my son grow up
because I have run out of luck

Will never find the X on the map
because there's two over my eyes
and I've been forced to take the nap.

{~The Capsule~}

December 1, 1969

The hand slowly reaches into the glass vase. I wish it wasn't clear so I didn't have to witness death approaching me on his black horse.

Please god, no, not me.

My entire existence being decided for me through a 25-inch box. I have no control, no say. A game of millimeters. The decrepit hand swills them around, teasing me, taunting me, haunting me.

No not that one, leave that one.

The hand pulls destiny out one by one. Almost ironic the date we were born will decide who gets to die.
September 14th, April 24th…
I see the fire in Death's eyes, the scythe swinging towards my head as the wrinkly hand rises out of the vase for the third time.

He opens up the blue capsule and unrolls the little piece of paper inside and I hear it. I see it. I feel it.

Time comes to a standstill. My entire short existence flashes before me. I vacate my body and zoom out to the edge of the universe. I kiss a beautiful butterfly lightly on the cheek and she lets out a tiny giggle as I am immediately zipped back into my body across the cosmos.

The words echo down a gigantic empty hallway. December 30th... December 30th... December 30th...

***

July 17th, 2014

"He didn't really say much when his birthday was called, he just sorta stared blankly at the TV. Course he wasn't much of a talker to begin with. Was probably a good few minutes and a couple other birthdays had already been called before he stood up off the couch and started pacing back and forth. Back and forth he went across the living room with his hands on his head, muttering to himself. I'd never seen him look that way before. A mix of scared, anxious, worried, nervous, and angry all wrapped into one. Could see his eyes were all red and watery. I tried to give him a hug but he wasn't having any of it. He ran off into the bedroom and slammed the door. Never did ask him what he was thinkin' or how he was feeling before he left on duty. Didn't have to. The answers were written all over his face."

- Rebecca Johnson, widow of

David William Johnson
Sergeant
15TH ADMIN CO, 1ST CAV DIV, USARV
Army of the United States
Fort Worth, Texas
December 30, 1950 to September 17, 1970

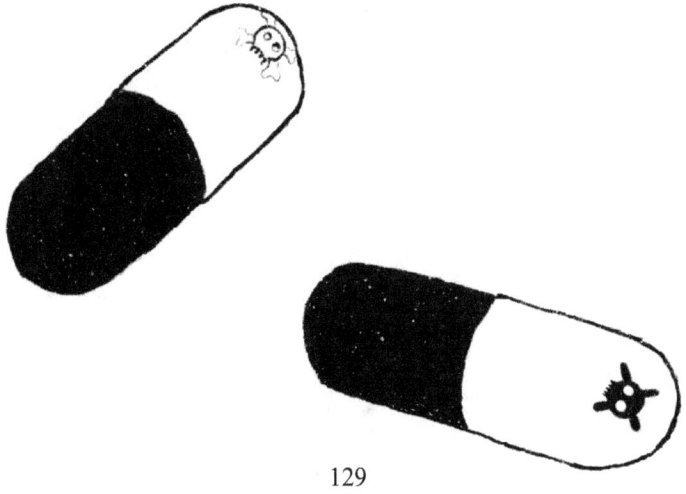

{~The Hall~}

Doors to his left, doors to his right.
The path ahead shrouded in light.

Each door labeled with a major life event.
I wish he knew what it all meant.

His birth, first words, and his first bike.
All so lovely in their own right.

As he continues down the hall,
the light fades to reveal them all.

I quickly cover the labels on each door,
yet the memories inside linger like a festering sore.

He opens each one; inside nothing but regrets.
Here take these pills, I hope he forgets.

It's not working, what do I do?
He's still remembering the labels;
I need them out of view.

His first date, proposal, and his wedding.
Make it stop there, we know where this is heading.

The night out, the drinks, the blurred lines behind the
wheel.
I had to take her in his place and he never did heal.

Here take these pills, you'll feel much better.
No not that many, and stop writing that letter.

So here he is at the end of the hall.
Finally found the door he's searched for most of all.

With a solemn heart I welcome you.
The door labeled *Exit,*
step on through.

131

{~The Duck~}

Tomorrow is crazy sock day at school. Momma just helped me pick a pair out at the store. Everyone is going to love them there sooooo cute. Momma looks sick though and very tired. She has these large dark circles around her eyes and she is walking very slowly down the aisles. Acting like a silly zombie. She sounds funny when she talks too and her hand feels all wet. I kinda don't wanna hold it anymore. I hope she's okay. I wish dad were here to take care of her.

On the drive home momma wouldn't let me turn the music up and she kept holding her head. Luckily, we stopped at her friend's house and she got some medicine. It took her forever inside the house to get it. I hope it cheers her up cuz she's Ms. Grumpy pants right now.

We are finally home and momma can't wait to take her medicine. She ran to the couch and started tearing it open. Never seen her face look like that before. So happy yet so sad at the same time. But then she got mad at me for some reason and yelled at me to go to bed.

I hope she feels better tomorrow cuz she's still a meany right now.

It's morning and I'm ready for school. Ready besides my socks for crazy sock day. Momma must still have them but she's not in her room. Oh, she fell asleep downstairs on the couch. She must have a crick in her neck from sleeping like that. Ew, she needs a bath, she smells like poo poo.

Momma wake up... She's so silly wearing one of my rubber ducky socks for school tied around her arm like that and not on her foot. Silly momma.

Wake up. Momma! Wake up!

Momma...

momma...

{~The Helmet~}

Built to serve and always protect,
shielding the mind is what I do best.

But when he saw the dancing lights behind,
the wind started to roar as he hit the red line.

The golden courage he once sported,
has turned into a blindfold; vision distorted.

The overseas demons he brought home on his
shoulders,
the lost brothers now just pictures in folders.

He drank to forget and never forgot to drink;
it lifted the weight, but still always on the brink.

Despite all the risk and all the warning,
this moment was inevitable; let's hope he sees morning.

I've been tested at speeds but none such as this,
the pavement is ugly, get away, I don't want to kiss.

As the smoke clears and the strobes circle round,
pieces of us scattered all around.

Like a fire through the forest; rapidly swarming.
The dam has burst and red lakes are forming.

I'm cracked and broken, just like my friend.
I've failed you, and this is the end.

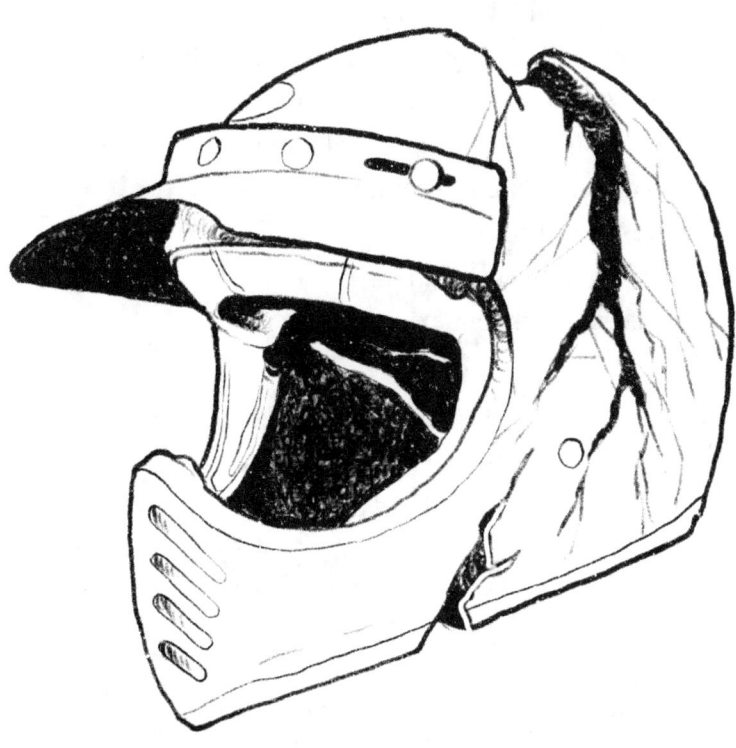

{~The Thesaurus~}

Complacently patient.
Arguably deficient.
Holding onto irregularities in the vast familiarities.
Defiantly devilish, making us dastardly dreadful.
Comatose with no antidote.
Plagues and perjury procreating the endless sickness.
Pulsating palpitations under asphyxiating pressures.
Insomnia inducing; dreams eluding.
Condemningly constricting.
Blue face suffocating.
Clawing at the desolation.
No need; imminent extinction.

-   *In other words, life sucks and then we die.*

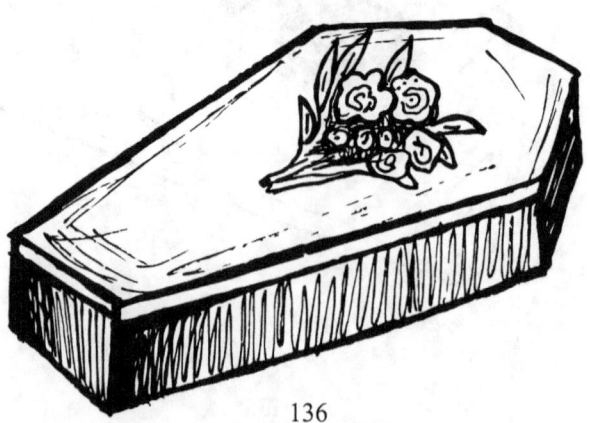

{~The Lump~}

There will be a last time you feel something is wrong.
There will be a last time he tells you
he's found something that doesn't belong.

There will be a last time they pump the poison into your
veins.
There will be a last time you spend all night clutching
the porcelain reins.

There will be a last time the fire engulfing your entire
body does ignite.
There will be a last time you force yourself to continue
the fight.

There will be a last time your eyes struggle to see our
faces.
There will be a last time you accept all of our embraces.

There will be a last time you have to hear our cries.
There will be a last time you say your goodbyes.

There will be a last time we hold your hands to pray.
There will be a last time we selfishly beg you to stay.

There will never be a time as broken as this.
There will never be a time that you aren't missed.

There will never be a time that we forget your name.
There will never be a time
we don't love you all the same.

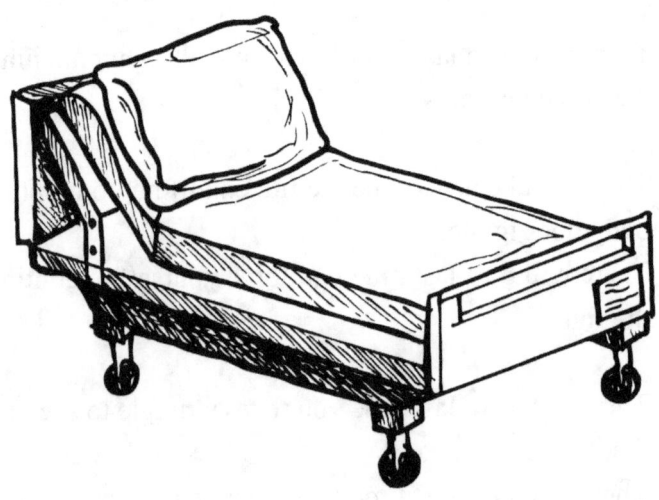

*It's sickening how quickly you became a stranger when you
moved out and into your new home in the ground.*

{~The Tree~}

You were there for my first birthday. You were actually older than me by a few weeks. I had you beat in size though old man. When I said my first words there you were. Probably chatting along with me; talking up this new storm we'd discovered together. You let me hug on you in a way I know now you hated, but you put up with me anyway. I didn't know any better and poked you in the eyes more than once. Thanks for not taking a chunk out of my hand. I know you could have easily.

When I had my tenth birthday you were there. Looking older but still youthful. You snuck your face onto the table when no one was looking and ate half the cake. It's okay I forgive you. Boy, at the time though I was mad at you. I didn't pet you for a whole like thirty minutes. When I got my first rejection from a girl I had a crush on, you were there waiting for me by the door like you were every day. Tail wagging; thumping a thousand times a second against the wall. You licked my face and reminded me about all the other girls that are out there.

When the burglar broke into our house you were there to protect us. You got him real good. Never seen your face look like that or those sounds come out of your mouth before. Never saw it again after that either.

When mom had to say goodbye to everyone you were there to comfort us all. I swear you knew something was wrong. You would push your way under my arm with your nose to lay comfy next to me. You would cry with me sometimes when I just couldn't take it anymore. I miss her too buddy...

When I left for college you were there trying to hop in the car to go with me. Trust me I would have let you if it was allowed. Dad needed you there with him anyway. The old man needed some company and I know yours is the best kind.

On my twentieth birthday when I came home to visit dad, you were still there. You could barely walk anymore... or see... or hear... but damn it, you were there. There to greet me at the front door just as you had done thousands of times before. Even with your senses fading you still knew it was me. I could tell if you could, you would have run around the house in excitement just like you used to.

I remember giving you the longest goodbye pet and gave you too many of your favorite treats before I left that day. Didn't want to believe it but I kinda figured that might be the last time I got to see you before you joined mom upstairs.

Sure enough, it was. I got the call that you took one of your long naps and decided to stay that way. It's alright, I'm sure you were so tired. Get some rest now old man.

You didn't quite make it to twenty-one with me. We were gonna be drinking buddies. Couple of old friends sitting on the porch, shootin' the breeze, having a cold one.

Don't tell anybody but I cried a few times for you. You were probably looking down laughing at me every time about that from your cloud in the sky.

We buried you in the backyard next to the porch. Your favorite place to "water" the yard. Planted a baby tree to mark your final resting place. A new family lives in that house now since dad decided to move to Florida. Sometimes I drive by and can see that tree; huge and flourishing from the street outside. Towering over the house from the backyard.

In a way you became that tree. You helped it grow up big and strong just as you did me. Your tired old bones became the trunk. Your soft fur became the bark. Your wagging excited tail became the leaves blowing in the wind. You're always looking over that family now, sheltering them from life's storms, just as you did ours for so long.

{~The Bird~}

- *Father*

"Why don't you go ahead and step back from the ledge there son."

- *Son*

"Why? Everybody wants to know what it's like to be able to fly."

- *Father*

"Yeah well, you're not a bird. You ain't got no wings. You can't fly. You'll just fall."

- *Son*

"Well maybe sometimes falling is better than flying anyway. Just depends on where you're trying to go and I'm just trying to go anywhere but here. Seems that fallin' is the fastest way to do just that."

- *Father*

"C'mon now, you can't do this to us... To your mother. She can't handle such a thing. Would crush her little heart. She loves you too much. *We* love you too much."

- *Son*

"Yeah well this ain't about you! Or mom! Or anybody else for that matter! And don't you f**kin' dare call me selfish. If you were in such terrible pain every second of every day and all you wanted to do was get up off your chair, turn off the TV, and leave. I would f**king hold the door for you on your way out. Not because I wanted to see you go, but because I know I couldn't possibly understand the pain you were experiencing. And I would never ask you to continue to endure it for me. That's not my right, and it's not yours now."

- *Father*

"Fine, don't do it for me, or for your mother, or for anyone else. Step back here for yourself and yourself only. No matter how bad you think you need to be down there living scattered among the rocks, as soon as the air is the only thing between you and them and you hear the deafening roar of the wind whistling past your ears, you're gonna god**mn wish you were a bird. Believe me son. Listen... your past experiences don't have to dictate your future actions."

● *Son*

"You don't get it. The past is who I am. It's all I am. It's on a chain around my ankle with no way to cut the steel. There is only one way to get rid of the past and that's to make sure there is no future..."

"You're right dad. I'm not a bird... and I ain't got no wings... and I'm so tired of painfully flapping my arms forcing myself to pretend that I do."

{~The Clock Pt.2~}

when we say that you were taken before *your time*
what we really mean is
we can't accept that it's *our time* to move on

{~The End~}

Stop striving to be something else other than the best version of you, you can be.

This life is brief, it can't be spent wanting to live someone else's.

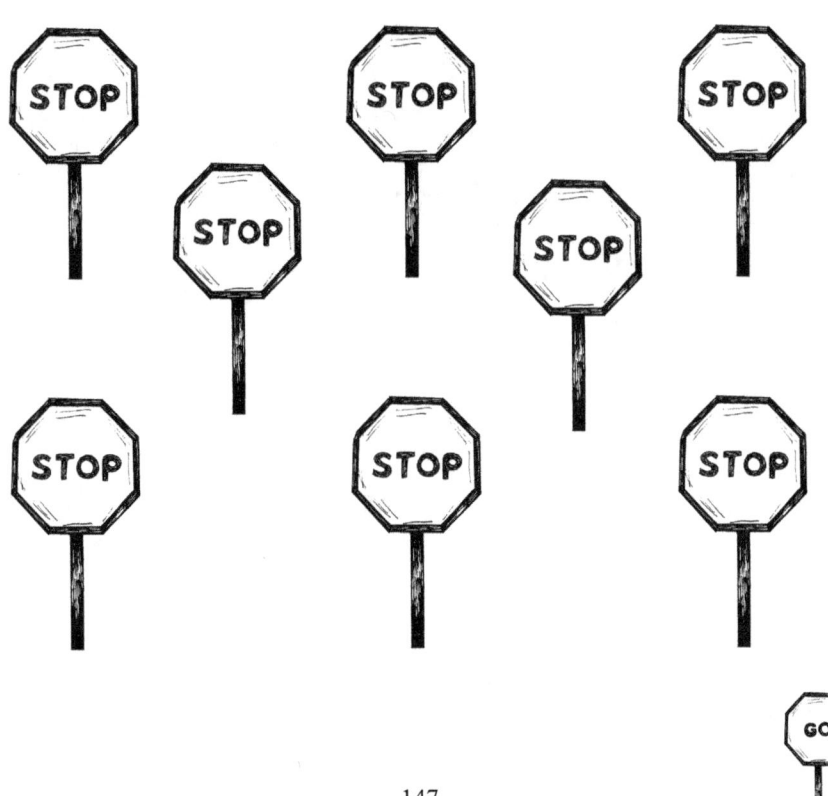

I would like to thank anyone that has impacted my life in any way, shape or form. For good or bad, better or worse. Without you this wouldn't have been possible.